On line   ries

The Shell Princess

Gwyneth Rees is half Welsh and half English and grew up in Scotland. She went to Glasgow University and qualified as a doctor in 1990. She is a child and adolescent psychiatrist, but has now stopped practising so that she can write full-time.

She is the author of many bestselling books, including the Fairies series, the Mermaid series, the Magic Princess Dress series, the My Super Sister series and the Cosmo series, as well as several books for older readers. She lives near London with her husband, Robert, and their daughters, Eliza and Lottie.

Books by Gwyneth Rees

Mermaid Magic
Rani's Sea Spell
The Shell Princess

Fairy Dust
Fairy Treasure
Fairy Dreams
Fairy Gold
Fairy Rescue
Fairy Secrets

Cosmo and the Magic Sneeze
Cosmo and the Great Witch Escape
Cosmo and the Secret Spell

The Shell Princess

Gwyneth Rees

Illustrated by Annabel Hudson

MACMILLAN CHILDREN'S BOOKS

First published 2001 by Macmillan Children's Books

This edition published 2016 by Macmillan Children's Books
an imprint of Pan Macmillan
20 New Wharf Road, London N1 9RR
Associated companies throughout the world
www.panmacmillan.com

ISBN 978-1-5098-1871-6

A CIP catalogue record for this book is available from
the British Library.

In memory of my father and grandfather

chapter one

Rani's long red hair streamed out behind her as she swam through the clear, warm water of Tingle Reef. She was going to visit her friend, Morva, who lived in a floating cave on the edge of the reef. To get there you had to swim past a sea-cactus with blue flowers and then carry on until you came to a needle-shaped bush which pointed up towards the magic rock where Morva lived.

Morva was a magic mermaid, just like Rani. Both of them had orange tails and

long red hair, unlike the other mermaids who had blonde hair and green tails. Morva had been teaching Rani how to use her special powers ever since Rani had discovered that she could do magic too.

As she entered Morva's cave, Rani stopped to stare at the painting on the wall. It showed a red-haired mermaid swimming down through what looked like a giant burst of golden light.

"You look thoughtful," said Morva, swimming up behind her.

"I was just wondering," Rani said, "if you ever miss your old home."

Although Morva had lived in Tingle Reef for a very long time, she had not been born there. She had grown up in a secret place, far away in the Deep Blue, where magic mermaids lived. The giant golden light in the picture was the entrance to the magic mermaids' home.

"Sometimes I do," Morva said. "Sometimes I dream about it."

"I wish I could remember it," sighed Rani.

Rani had been found in Tingle Reef

as a baby – inside a Giant Clam-Shell – and she had lived there ever since. She had been adopted by a family who she loved very much, but she had always felt curious about the place she had really come from.

"That mermaid looks *so* beautiful," Rani said, still gazing at the picture. "I hope I look like her when I grow up."

"Perhaps you'll look like me," Morva teased.

"Oh, no!" said Rani at once. "I could never look as beautiful as you!"

Morva's red hair stretched to the tip of her tail and shone so brightly that Morva could always be spotted in dark water from a long way away. Not that the water in Tingle Reef was ever dark – it was a lovely clear blue colour which made the reef such a wonderful place to live. But Rani had made a few trips with Morva into the Deep Blue, and she had noticed that the darker the water became, the more Morva's hair seemed to glow.

"Just like my pendant," Rani thought, looking down at it. Rani's amber pendant was a gift from her grandmother, and it seemed to glow against Rani's skin. It wasn't just any necklace – it was a message-stone. *Her* message-stone. Magic mermaids use message-stones to see their families when they became separated from them. Rani had learned by looking into her message-stone that her true parents had died when she was a baby, but that she had a twin brother. When she looked in her message-stone and saw his red hair and twinkly eyes looking back at her, she could hardly wait to meet him.

"Morva, *when* will you take me there?" Rani asked, gazing longingly at the painting.

"I told you, Rani," Morva replied. "When your magic is stronger."

"But my magic is strong now," Rani protested. "I've been practising really hard. Look!" And she closed her eyes and concentrated on turning the water in Morva's cave from crystal clear to bright pink. When she opened her eyes the water was orange.

"Oh dear," Morva laughed, quickly

turning it back again.

Rani felt silly and feeling silly made her cross. "It's not fair!" she said, banging the end of her tail impatiently against the floor of the cave. "*Why* do I have to keep waiting?"

Morva stopped laughing. Rani was usually very good-tempered. "I didn't

realize it was upsetting you so much, Rani," she said gently. "I know how hard you've been practising your magic and it's getting stronger all the time. But I didn't think there was any need to rush. I thought you were happy here in Tingle Reef."

"I *am* happy here," replied Rani. "But I really want to meet *him*!" She held the pendant in her hands and looked inside at the face of her brother. "He misses me just as much, I know he does. I have to find him!"

"Listen carefully, Rani," Morva said, looking at her gravely. "The first thing you have to realize is that your brother may not be where we think he is. If your parents put you inside a Giant

Clam-Shell in order to keep you safe, they probably did the same with your brother. He might not have been found by his own people. Like you, he may have been adopted by a different group of mermaids, and if so he could be anywhere."

Rani shook her head. "Morva, I just know he got back safely," she said. "I can *feel* it."

Morva paused, as if she was thinking really hard about something. "There's something else you should know," she said. "Another reason you might not be ready to make the journey back yet." She swam over to the painting and placed her hand over the place where the golden light seemed to be rising out of the seabed. "Watch carefully," she commanded.

As Rani watched, a gold line started to appear all by itself, on top of the picture. "What is it?" she gasped.

"Look more carefully," Morva told her, as the line spread.

Rani swam back to look at the gold

lines from a greater distance, and then she knew. "It's a map!" she said. "A golden map."

"That's right," Morva nodded. "This map shows us the way home."

She lifted her hand from the wall and the lines instantly disappeared.

"Bring it back!" gasped Rani. "We need it to find our way there."

"I remember the way quite clearly. I don't need a map," Morva replied. "But the map has another purpose."

Rani frowned. "What do you mean?"

"Any mermaid can follow a map and swim across the Deep Blue," Morva said. "But only a magic mermaid can swim through the golden light to get to our home. And if a mermaid can make the map appear, then it means her magic power is strong enough to let her in."

"Please, can I try?" asked Rani excitedly.

"The magic in the hand that touches the picture must be very strong in order for the map to show itself," Morva warned her. "If you try too soon, you may be disappointed."

"I still want to see if I can do it," Rani said.

"Very well," Morva said, moving back from the wall. "If you *really* want to put your magic to the test . . ."

Chapter Two

Slowly, Rani placed her hand flat against the picture on Morva's wall. Nothing happened at first, then she felt her hand starting to tingle.

"Look," she whispered, holding in her breath as gold lines began to appear on the cave wall. "I've done it!"

Morva nodded slowly.

"So my magic *is* strong enough!" Rani said, turning her head to look at Morva. "Does that mean I'm ready to visit my brother?"

"In a way, yes," Morva replied carefully. "But there are different ways of being ready, Rani. Are you sure you're ready to leave your family? And are *they* ready for you to go?"

Rani frowned. The truth was that she hadn't told her family anything about this yet.

"I'm sure they'll let me," she said. "I'll go and ask them now!"

But as she swam back towards her own cave, she started to worry. What if her family were against the idea? Her parents could be so protective of her sometimes, especially her mother. She couldn't just leave Tingle Reef without telling them. She loved them too much to do that. She sighed. She would just have to *make* them see how important it was for her to make this trip, that was all!

When Rani got back home to their cave, her mother, Miriam, was cooking dinner while her father, Murdoch, bounced her baby sister, Pearl, on the end of his tail. Rani's other sister, Kai, was peering into the cooking pot and complaining that they were having seaweed *again*. "Mother, Father, Kai . . . I've got something to tell you," Rani began.

But before she could continue, there was a knock on the wall outside and four long wriggly arms pushed back their seaweed-flap.

"Good day, everyone," said Octavius

the octopus, as he peered in through one of the gaps he had made in the seaweed curtain. "May I come in?"

"Of course," said Murdoch. "Though we're just about to have dinner."

Rani noticed that her mother was frowning. Octavius had a habit of visiting at inconvenient times and staying for ages.

"I've already had my dinner," Octavius said, settling himself on the most comfortable rock. "Some of my delicious stew. Do you know, I don't believe I've ever tasted anything as fine as my very own cooking? I don't know why I should be such a talented cook – unless it's another consequence of having such a large brain. I suppose I *am* able to put a lot of thought into my recipes."

Rani felt impatient. Once Octavius got started on the subject of his brain, he was impossible to stop. She would never get to speak to her family at this rate. Then she had an idea. As Octavius continued to boast, Rani decided to try out some magic. As she focused on him she could feel her magic struggling against a very strong force indeed. She concentrated extra-hard, and was beginning to feel a bit dizzy, when something weird started to happen. Golden sparks appeared around Octavius's mouth as he said, "Of course, my brain is really just of average size for an octopus."

Miriam and Murdoch stared at him in disbelief and Kai nearly dropped the shell-cutlery she was putting on the table.

"And in any case," continued Octavius, "quantity does not always mean quality." And he gave them a humble smile as he exited their cave.

"I don't believe it!" gasped Miriam.

They all started to laugh.

Rani decided that now was as good a time as any to break her news. "Mother, Father, Kai . . ." she began again firmly, and this time they all turned to listen.

"A magic stone?" frowned Miriam, when Rani had finished. "I don't understand."

"It's a *message*-stone, Mother," Rani said. "Morva showed me how to open the pendant and we found out that my real parents must have died when I was a baby. They were in some sort of danger and that was why they put me inside the Clam-Shell. But I had a twin brother and they put him inside another shell or something because he's still alive."

Rani's mother sat on the seaweed mat, looking dazed. "And now you want to leave us in order to find him?"

"I don't *want* to leave you," Rani said, "but I have to find my brother. You can't come with me because only magic mermaids can go to the place Morva comes from."

"It sounds far too dangerous," Miriam said. "And you are too young to make such a big journey. Perhaps when you're older—"

"It's not dangerous!" Rani protested. "Morva will be with me. Please, Mother, I'm ready to go *now*!"

But her mother was shaking her head firmly.

Rani looked at her father. Surely Murdoch would understand. "Father?" she pleaded. "Please say I can go!"

"We think of you as belonging here with us, Rani," Murdoch said gently, "that's the problem." He sighed. "I'm afraid I agree with your mother. I don't want you to go either. You don't know what you will find there, Rani. It may not make you happy. And we don't want to lose you."

"You won't lose me," Rani said, fighting back tears. Why couldn't they understand? They *had* to let her go! Otherwise *she* was going to lose her brother!

Chapter Three

Rani's pet sea horse, Roscoe, was swinging himself on one of the seaweed swings in the shell-garden. He looked a bit huffy when Rani approached and flipped himself round on the swing so that he had his back to her.

Rani realized that she hadn't spent much time with Roscoe recently – she'd been too busy practising her magic.

"I'm sorry, Roscoe," Rani said, stroking his bony head. "I haven't been a very good friend lately – have I?"

"No, you haven't," Roscoe said crossly. But he couldn't help smiling when Rani tickled his neck. He turned around and listened as Rani explained what had just happened.

"So . . ." said Roscoe, when she had finished. "You don't want to lose *this* family but you can't bear not to find your

other family as well. That seems fair enough to me!"

"Try telling that to Mother and Father," Rani sighed.

Roscoe looked thoughtful. "We need to think of a way of making them see this from your point of view," he said.

"Yes, but how?" Rani asked him.

Roscoe thought about it. "I know! Who has more clever thoughts in one day than you mermaids have in a whole year?"

"Octavius," Rani replied. "At least, that's what he's always *saying*, but—"

"Exactly. *This* is his chance to prove his point," Roscoe interrupted her. "We'll tell him the problem and he'll *have* to come up with an idea just to prove to us how clever he is!"

"But what if it isn't a *good* idea?" Rani asked nervously.

"So?" Roscoe said, flicking her with his tail as he jumped off the swing. "Do you have *any* ideas *at all*?"

Rani shook her head.

"Well, come on, then!" And the little sea horse bobbed ahead of her towards Octavius's cave.

As soon as Roscoe tapped his bony tail against the cave wall to be let in, the octopus yelled at them to go away. "You know I always rest my brain at this time of the day!" he shouted.

Rani sighed. Still, at least that meant that Octavius had returned to his usual self.

"Octavius, this is an emergency!" shouted the sea horse. "Rani needs your help."

"Rani?" Octavius grumbled as he swam over to his seaweed-flap and lifted it up. "Can't she use her magic to sort it out, whatever it is? I'm really very tired."

"This isn't a problem for magic," Roscoe continued perkily. "This is a problem that can only be solved by some clever *thinking*."

"Well, really," grunted the octopus.

"*Very* clever thinking, Octavius," Roscoe repeated, and paused dramatically. "That's why we've come to you."

"I see. Hmm," Octavius looked flustered. "Well, I suppose you'd better

come in and tell me what the problem is.
I'll certainly have some clever thoughts
about it – but my clever thoughts can
sometimes be *too* clever to actually put
into action, you understand." He
coughed.

"Octavius, I don't know what to
do . . ." Rani began to explain her
problems.

As Octavius listened, his big forehead
formed a very crinkly brow.

"I've got to persuade Mother and
Father to let me go, or I'll never get to
meet my brother," Rani finished, starting
to cry.

"Oh dear, oh dear," muttered
Octavius, who was really very soft-
hearted when it came to mermaids

crying. He placed all his arms round Rani in a very complicated hug.

"You look like you're trapped inside a cage of octopus-arms," Roscoe joked, trying to cheer her up.

And it was then that it happened. Octavius grunted out loud as the idea hit him. It was a very clever idea – the

cleverest he'd ever had!

"Leave it to me," he told Rani, extracting his arms one by one. "You go back home and wait for me. I won't be long. I just have to make something first."

And he dashed outside his cave, churning up the water in his hurry.

Later on that day, Rani's family were sitting quietly in their cave. Things had felt very tense when Rani returned although no one had said any more about her request to leave Tingle Reef. It seemed that as far as her parents were concerned, the matter was closed. Kai was hardly speaking to her, though, and even Pearl seemed to sense that something was wrong, refusing to settle down to sleep even with Rani's mother singing to her.

Pearl had just about dropped off when Octavius arrived. He was carrying a strange contraption which he set down proudly on the floor of the cave.

"I have to show you this," he said. "It's a special cage. I made it out of razor shells and spider-glue – and the mesh is made out of bind-weed. A very clever invention, don't you think?"

"What's it for?" Miriam asked.

"I'm going to use it to catch a magic fish!" Octavius said. "They live way out in the Deep Blue and are said to be very beautiful indeed. A whole shoal of them is coming to visit Morva tomorrow."

"But, Octavius, you can't trap a magic fish here," Miriam protested. "It wouldn't be fair."

"Why not? I really want one for a pet. You have Roscoe, don't you?"

"That's different," said Murdoch. "Roscoe *chooses* to live with us. You can't keep a magic fish here against its will."

"Hmm," said Octavius, pretending to

31

think about it. "What do you think, Rani?"

Before she could reply, Miriam turned on Octavius, her eyes flashing angrily. "Is this your clumsy way of telling us that you think we should let Rani go with Morva?"

Octavius turned a bit pink. "Well, she did come to me in great distress and I do think—"

Miriam turned away from him to face Rani. "You went to Octavius to ask for help?"

Rani nodded. "But, Mother—"

"Well, all I can say, Rani," Miriam interrupted her crisply, "is that in that case you must have felt pretty desperate!"

"I beg your pardon—" began Octavius huffily.

"She didn't mean it like that, Octavius," Murdoch hastily intervened. "We're just shocked that Rani feels so strongly about this that she chose to go to someone outside the family about it, that's all." He paused.

There was an awkward silence.

Finally Rani's mother spoke. "I don't ever want your home to feel like a prison to you, Rani," she said, staring at Octavius's cage. "If you need to find this other place so badly – and if Morva will be there to look after you – then . . ." – she looked at her husband to check that he agreed – ". . . Then perhaps we should think about letting you go."

"Oh, Mother, thank you!" gasped Rani, rushing to give her a hug.

"But *if* we let you go with Morva, you must promise to come back to us!" Miriam added sharply.

"Of course I'll come back," laughed Rani. She turned to her sister. "Kai – no other sister could ever be as good as you! When I find my brother, I know he'll want you to be *his* sister too!"

"Oh, dear me," said Octavius, dabbing at his eyes with an old piece of seaweed. Mermaids were so *emotional*! Honestly, if it wasn't for him and his clever thinking, then goodness knows *what* would become of them all!

Chapter four

Rani couldn't believe she was really going with Morva.

Morva was excited too when she came to collect her. "I can't wait to see my old home again!" she beamed.

Rani and her family took ages saying goodbye, so that Morva began to wonder if they were ever going to leave at all, but eventually, after a final round of hugs, the two mermaids set off.

"We are going further away than you could possibly imagine, Rani," Morva told her, when they were finally out of sight of Tingle Reef. "This is like no other journey you have ever made before. We will be travelling further into the Deep Blue than any Tingle Reef mermaid has *ever* travelled." She paused. "First, though, we have to swim a lot faster. I believe it's time to use some magic!"

And all that anyone watching would have seen after that, were two streaks of gold light speeding through the water.

"This is where we catch our whale," Morva said, finally stopping at a very unusual-looking rock with several mermaid-sized seats chiselled out of it. "This is a whale-stop. We must sit and wait."

"A *whale-stop*?" Rani repeated, in disbelief.

"That's right. I'm not talking about your average whale. I'm talking about the Giant Whales who live out in the Deep Blue," Morva explained. "They have always been friends to us magic mermaids."

Morva started to make some strange whale-calling noises, and soon two huge white eyes appeared next to the rock, making Rani jump. The sea was so dark that it was hard to see the rest of the creature's body.

Morva reached out and patted the whale's nose, which was the same size as her hand. "Did you have trouble finding us? My whale-calls are a bit

rusty, I'm afraid."

The whale told them that his name was Jonah and that he had seen their hair shining from a long way away. Rani saw that his head was so huge that, if he opened his mouth, he could easily have devoured them both in one bite. "Where are you going?" he asked. "Home?"

Morva nodded. "Have you room for two of us?"

"I expect so – if you're careful. Swim inside."

"Thank you. Come on, Rani," Morva said, easing herself off the rock.

"Swim inside *what?*" asked Rani.

"Why, inside Jonah's mouth, of course. Look – he's opened it for us." Morva swam in and beckoned for Rani to follow. "Come on, Rani. You know very well that whales only eat plankton."

Rani still felt a bit unsure as she slowly swam in between the whale's huge jaws to join her friend. Rani saw that the whale didn't have any teeth but had a bony sieve inside its mouth which it used to sift out plankton from the water.

"Now," said Morva. "You must keep very still – no splashing around or he'll get cross with us."

"I'll keep *very* still," Rani promised, not relishing the idea of Jonah getting cross with her while she was sitting inside his mouth.

Rani soon discovered that there was nothing to be alarmed about. The whale's mouth was soft and warm, and the journey from then on was quite comfortable. His mouth was shut so they couldn't see where they were going but that didn't seem to worry Morva.

Soon Rani fell asleep and started to dream that she was back in Tingle Reef with all her family – but her brother was there too. It was such a happy dream that she didn't want to wake up when Morva finally shook her gently and told her that they had to get out.

"Why? Are we there already?" Rani asked, thinking that perhaps she had been asleep for longer than she'd thought.

"No, but Jonah has stopped. There's some sort of problem. Now, stay close to me, Rani. This part of the Deep Blue is very dark and it's very easy to get lost."

As they swam out of Jonah's mouth, Rani shivered because the water here was so cold.

"What's wrong?" Morva asked the whale.

Jonah told them to swim underneath his belly and look down.

They swam under and saw that they were very close to the seabed.

"It's a shark!" Rani gasped, pointing below them to a long black fish with a huge pointed nose and sharp white teeth. The shark was nudging something that looked like a white furry ball.

"What's it got?" Rani whispered, starting to swim closer.

Morva pulled her back. "Be careful.

We don't want it to see us."

The white ball – whatever it was – was making sobbing noises. Suddenly a little black nose became visible, then two blue eyes and two little white ears.

"I don't believe it," Morva gasped. "It's a bear cub!"

"A *bear cub*!" Rani repeated. She had heard stories about the Great White Swimming Bears that lived on the other side of the Deep Blue but she had never seen one before. "What's it doing here?"

"That shark must have caught it," Morva said.

At that moment three more sharks appeared – another adult one and two youngsters. "Dad, what's for dinner?" one of the young ones demanded.

"We're starving!"

"This," the biggest shark replied, prodding the whimpering bear cub. "And we have to eat it straight away before its mother comes looking for it."

"Morva – we've got to *do* something!" gasped Rani, as the little bear looked towards them helplessly.

"Do you remember that tasting spell I taught you?" Morva whispered. "The one that you tried on Kai, that made her think seaweed tasted delicious?"

Rani nodded. How could she ever forget the day Kai had asked for a second helping of greens? "But how will that help?"

"I'll do it in reverse," Morva said. "Watch." And as Morva closed her eyes and concentrated, Rani saw little gold sparks beginning to appear around the mouth of the biggest shark as he sank his teeth into the bear cub's white fur.

The shark let out a snort of disgust and dropped the little bear before he had even taken a bite. "Yuck!" he said, spitting out a bit of fur. "That tastes horrible."

The other sharks were frowning. Baby bear was normally delicious.

Just then an angry roar sounded from above.

"MUMMY!" shouted the little bear cub. "I'm down here!"

A furious mother bear came charging down through the water, her white fur standing on end as she growled in rage.

She lashed out with her sharp claws at the sharks, who quickly panicked and swam off.

Rani waved as she and Morva watched the mother bear and her cub paddle away. The little bear kept turning back to look at the two mermaids, as if he couldn't believe his eyes.

"Where do swimming bears live?" Rani asked.

"Nobody knows for certain," Morva said, leading the way back to where Jonah was waiting for them. "Except that to get there you have to keep swimming up until you can't swim any further. Mermaids get dizzy if they swim that high, which is why nobody's ever been there."

"Now, Rani," Morva said, when they were safely back inside Jonah's warm mouth. "I want you to try and get some rest now."

Rani soon fell asleep and this time she dreamed she was swimming in sparkling water where big furry white bears swam along lazily beside her.

chapter five

"Wake up, Rani," Morva said, poking her. "We're here."

"*Where?*" Rani asked dozily, and then she remembered. She was about to meet her brother. And not just in a dream!

As Jonah opened his mouth for them to swim out, she blinked because the sea outside was full of a bright light. "It looks like . . . It looks like . . ." she gasped, but she couldn't continue because she had never seen anything like this before.

They were right on the sea-bottom
and in front of them there seemed to be
an opening in the seabed, from which a
gold surge of light rose upwards through
the water. The water all around glowed
and Rani held up her arms to shield her
eyes from the glare.

"Don't cover your eyes, Rani," Morva

told her. "You must look into the brightness. It won't hurt you."

Slowly, Rani looked. Her eyes seemed to be getting used to the bright water and she started to feel a strong tingling sensation in her skin.

"You've been wonderful, Jonah!" Morva said, swimming up to kiss him on the nose. Rani felt too shy to give him a kiss so she thanked him and gave him a pat instead.

As Jonah swam upwards and disappeared, Morva took hold of Rani's hand. "Your magic normally starts from inside you, Rani," she explained. "That's why you feel it in your belly button first. But now the magic is all around you. How do you feel?"

"I feel . . . strange," Rani said.

Morva smiled. "Now comes the strangest bit of all. We must swim down through that golden beam into that hole in the seabed."

"B-but . . ." Rani stammered. "There is nothing under the seabed." She had always been taught that the seabed was where everything ended.

"If you are a magic mermaid, it is different," Morva said gently. "Come with me."

And together they swam right into the beam of golden light. Rani felt warm inside and out. The tingling she usually felt in her fingers when she did magic felt as though it had taken over her whole body. She tried to speak but found that no words came.

"*Think* your thoughts to me, Rani," Rani could hear Morva saying inside her head. Thought-reading was part of her magic. "We will be able to speak to each other again when we have passed through the magic light."

The light was so strong that Rani could hardly see Morva as they swam downwards. As the brightness gradually lessened, Rani saw that she was swimming through a golden passageway under the seabed. "Wow!" she gasped.

"I know," said Morva, speaking out loud again. "I had forgotten how beautiful it was."

"But where does it lead to?" Rani asked.

"Wait and see," Morva smiled.

Eventually the passageway opened out into a huge cave. The cave was empty but the walls were decorated with pictures of mermaids swimming – all of them with red hair. They could hear voices now.

"This way," said Morva, and she swam over to an arched opening in the cave wall. "Through here," she said, swimming through and disappearing.

For a moment Rani felt nervous. Then she too swam through the archway and found herself in the most beautiful garden she could ever have dreamed of.

She had never seen flowers like these before – as tall as mermaids, with huge petals of bright colours. Huge oyster shells lazed about, proudly displaying their pearls for everyone to see, and beautiful golden fish swam between the feathery plants, playing hide and seek with each other. But what Rani couldn't stop staring at were the mermaids themselves. They all had orange tails – some tipped with gold – and every one of them had red hair like Rani's.

A young mermaid swam over, looking at them curiously. "Who are you?" she asked.

"I am Morva," Morva told her, looking as if she expected this to make some sort of impression, which it obviously did not.

"I'm Rani," Rani added quickly. "We're from Tingle Reef."

"Where's that?" asked the mermaid.

"A very long way away from here," Morva said, staring round at the other mermaids to see if she recognized any of them. "Perhaps you can help us. I need to speak to an *old* person – a *very* old person, you understand."

The young mermaid peered into Morva's eyes as if she had only just noticed that Morva was a lot older than she had first thought. "I'll take you to the Mer-King," she said. "He's *ancient!*"

"That will do very nicely," Morva said smiling.

Rani kept a sharp look-out for her brother as she followed closely behind her friend. They were led into another passageway and through into another cave and out again into a large courtyard.

"The Mer-King's palace is that way," the mermaid said, pointing to a pathway of golden shells. "Just follow those."

Rani and Morva thanked her and swam along until the shells came to an end a short distance away from the entrance to a very grand cave. Two rock pillars had been erected outside the arched cave-opening and a merman with a smart seaweed belt stood guard outside.

"Come on," whispered Morva. "Let's see if the Mer-King knows your brother."

And trembling a little, Rani waited as Morva swam forward and requested permission to be let inside.

chapter Six

After the guard had sent a messenger
inside the palace, Morva came back to
wait with Rani.

"What if the Mer-King won't see us?"
Rani asked, trying not to flick up any of
the golden shells accidentally with her
tail.

"Oh, he'll see us," Morva said
confidently.

And at that moment, an old merman
appeared, staring at them from the
palace entrance. His red hair was

streaked with white and he had a gold seaweed crown on his head. "Someone said that Morva was here!" he boomed out.

Morva swam forward, smiling. "She is."

The Mer-King stared into her eyes in disbelief. "*Morva!*" he exclaimed. "After all these years!" And he grabbed her hand and squeezed it excitedly. "Nobody knew what became of you! Come in! Come in! You must tell me everything!"

"Wait," said Morva, motioning for Rani to come forward. "I have brought someone with me. This is my friend Rani."

"You are very welcome, Rani," the Mer-King beamed at her. "Now you

must both come inside." And he led the way back into the palace.

"You *know* him?" Rani hissed to Morva, under her breath, as they followed him past the two massive pillars.

"Oh yes," smiled Morva. "We were great friends!"

"I was a very handsome Mer-Prince in those days, Rani," the Mer-King said, turning round to wink at her. "Can you imagine that?"

"Well . . ." Rani said, blushing, and the king laughed.

The palace was made out of many interconnecting caves, none of which seemed all that grand, until the king led them through a small archway into his main chamber. A carpet of gold moss covered the floor and the walls were a sparkly blue that reminded Rani of the water in Tingle Reef. Gold and silver fish of all sizes swam around inside the room and gold seaweed was strung from the ceiling. In the centre of the room, a silver dish was piled high with the most delicious-looking sea-fruits imaginable.

There were several soft seaweed cushions scattered about the floor, and the Mer-King flopped down on one and stretched out his tail with a sigh. "Sit down, sit down!" he urged them. "The Mer-Queen is out at the moment but she will be back soon. You must dine with us. You must be hungry after your long journey."

He snapped his fingers and ordered

some refreshments while they waited.

"Who did you marry?" Morva asked him. "No – let me guess!" And she reeled off a whole list of names that meant absolutely nothing to Rani. Morva began to ask about each of her old friends in turn, until Rani grew quite bored. If only there was somebody here to play with! Rani's ears pricked up as she heard Morva ask, "Do you have any children?"

The Mer-King looked sad. "We had a son – but he died a long time ago in a sea-quake." He quickly attempted to smile. "But this is a happy day! Let us not talk of sad things."

Rani was longing to ask the Mer-King if he knew her brother but Morva was asking so many questions that she couldn't get a word in.

Morva started to tell the Mer-King about Tingle Reef and about Rani turning up as a baby inside a Giant Clam-Shell. "Nobody knew that she was a magic mermaid, except me," said Morva. "And I have always promised her that one day I would bring her here." Morva leaned over and touched Rani's amber pendant. "We didn't know anything about her true family at all – until we found this."

"A message-stone," the Mer-King said, looking at Rani more closely.

"Yes – and inside Rani found a picture of her parents and learned that they had died when she was a baby. But there was another baby inside the stone – a boy who we know is the same age now as Rani. So I have explained to Rani that she must have a twin brother . . ." Morva paused. "And we were hoping that he might be here."

The Mer-King was staring intently at Rani now. "May I see the picture of this boy?" he asked.

Rani removed the stone from her neck and gently blew on it. As they watched, the surface softened and her brother's face appeared, looking out at her from inside.

The Mer-King looked over her shoulder at the face of the boy and gasped, "I don't believe it!"

"Do you know him?" asked Morva.

"This is my grandson," the Mer-King said, putting a hand on Rani's shoulder and turning her to face him.

Rani felt her heart start to beat faster. If this was true . . . If her twin brother was really the Mer-King's grandson, then that meant . . .

The Mer-King was looking at her with tears in his eyes now. "I-I can't believe it," he stammered, as he touched her with a trembling hand. "Rani – you must be the lost Shell Princess!"

Rani and Morva listened as the Mer-King told them how his son and his son's young wife had been on a trip in the Deep Blue when they had sent a message saying that they would have to delay their return home because their baby was about to arrive.

"We went to find them," the Mer-King said, "but by the time we got there, a terrible sea-quake had destroyed the whole of the seabed where they were. We thought they had all been killed until we came across a Giant Clam-Shell. My grandson was inside. He was just a few days old. They must have put him inside the shell to protect him. He had a message-stone round his neck – just like yours, Rani. We couldn't look inside the stone until he was old enough to open it for us. When he told us he could see a little girl smiling at him, we thought he was making it up. But then we looked and, sure enough, there was this little red-haired mer-girl smiling out at us, with a face exactly like her mother's. We searched everywhere we could think of. We searched for years. But in the end we were forced to stop looking . . ."

The Mer-King touched Rani's hair. "I should have recognized you straight away," he told her. "But I have not looked at your picture for a very long time. It upset me to be reminded that my little granddaughter was out there somewhere all alone."

"Oh, but I wasn't alone—" Rani started to tell him, but she was interrupted by the palace messenger.

"The Mer-Queen and the Mer-Prince have returned," he announced.

At that moment an excited voice shouted, "Grandfather!" and a boy of Rani's age, with short red hair and sparkling eyes, came swimming into the room. "Guess what—" He stopped short when he saw Rani and Morva.

"Let me introduce my grandson," the Mer-King said. "Rani, this is Peri."

"Hello," the boy said, looking a bit dazed as he slowly took in Rani's face, her hair and, finally, her amber pendant.

Rani swallowed. She found that she couldn't speak properly. "I'm-I'm . . ." she stammered.

Peri flipped his tail in excitement. "I know who you are! You're the girl in my pendant!" And he dived forward and grabbed Rani by the hands. "You're my *sister*, aren't you?"

Rani nodded as Peri started to spin her non-stop around the room.

"Peri, calm down!" his grandfather called out. "You'll make Rani dizzy."

"It's OK!" Rani laughed, looking lovingly into her brother's eyes. "I don't mind!"

And Rani knew that she wouldn't be able to stop feeling giddy today, even if she tried.

Chapter Seven

Rani and Peri spent the next few days getting to know each other. The longer they spent together, the more they liked each other, and soon they felt that they had never been separated at all.

"It helped being able to see you inside my message-stone," Peri told her. "I used to talk to you all the time so it was sort of like having you with me. But it's much better now because you can talk back!"

Rani laughed. "Ever since I first saw you inside *my* message-stone, I've been longing to meet you! I can't believe I'm really here with you. I keep thinking I must be dreaming and that I'll wake up and find myself back in Tingle Reef."

"Tingle Reef sounds a wonderful place," Peri said. "And you're so lucky having a mother and a father."

Rani agreed that she *was* lucky. "But the Mer-King and Queen are so kind," she said. "So *you're* lucky too!"

That night, the Mer-King and his wife were throwing a royal banquet in honour of their granddaughter and everyone was invited.

"You'll get to meet all my friends," Peri said, as he began to list them.

Rani started to think about all her friends in Tingle Reef. How was Roscoe getting on without her? And Octavius? And when she thought about Kai she got a funny little ache right in her middle, as if a part of her was missing.

That evening as everyone gathered in the palace, Morva was looking especially beautiful in a multi-coloured top with gold tassels. Her hair seemed even shinier than it had done in Tingle Reef. Rani could see that she was very happy to be back home again.

"Don't you miss your lobsters and your starfish?" she whispered, as she waited in line beside Morva, shaking hands with all the guests as they arrived.

"A little, but, oh . . . Rani . . . I can't help wishing that I'd come back years ago!"

"But then I would never have discovered who I really was," Rani reminded her. "And you wouldn't have been able to teach me all that magic!"

"That's true," Morva smiled. "But I've been thinking, Rani – you don't need me to teach you any more."

"Yes, I do!" protested Rani.

"No, you don't. You are strong enough to manage by yourself from now on. And that's why . . . I've decided to stay here."

"What?" Rani gasped. "But you promised Mother and Father you'd take me back!"

"I promised them I'd get you back *safely* – and I will. But, Rani, this is my true home – not Tingle Reef. I don't have any family to go back to. And after all, I can always go back and visit."

"You can do that too, Rani," the Mer-King added, overhearing them. "You can go back and visit your friends in Tingle Reef whenever you like."

"Oh, but I shan't need to *visit* them," Rani said, feeling confused. "I'll be going back there to stay."

"But you have found your real home now – and your real family," the Mer-King said. "Doesn't that make a difference?"

"My *real* home is in Tingle Reef," Rani protested. "And Mother and Father and Kai and Pearl *are* my real family!"

The Mer-King frowned and it was clear that he didn't agree.

"I have an idea," said Morva thoughtfully. "The message-stone will always show a magic mermaid her true family when she is separated from them. If, in your heart, you believe that your family in Tingle Reef is your true family, Rani . . ." – she pointed to Rani's pendant – "Well, why don't you look inside and see?"

Rani lifted up her pendant. She hadn't even opened the stone since she had met Peri.

As Rani blew on the stone and saw its hard shiny surface turn soft and watery, she started to smile.

"Are they there?" asked Morva.

Rani nodded. And as she gazed happily at the four familiar faces, she knew that it was time for her to go back to them.

"I'll come back and visit you, I promise," Rani said to Peri, who was upset when she told him her plans. Then she had a better idea. "I know! Why don't you come back with me and visit Tingle Reef?"

Peri asked the Mer-King, who thought it was a splendid idea.

"I shall send you both back in my special carriage. You will be quite safe because my dolphins will take care of you!"

And so it was settled. The only thing left to do was say goodbye to Morva.

"I'll really miss you," Rani said,

hugging her friend, as they waited for the royal carriage to arrive. "Are you sure you won't come with us? What about your floating cave? And what will I tell Octavius?"

"My floating cave can be my holiday home," Morva said brightly. "I intend to come back and visit you all soon – you can tell Octavius that!"

"Thank you for everything, Morva," Rani said. "I don't know what I'd have done if you hadn't been there to help me."

"Well, you might not have discovered all this . . ." Morva admitted. "But tell me, Rani, now that you *have* found it, won't it make you *unhappy* having to give it up?"

"I won't be giving it up," Rani told her, smiling. "I'll be coming back again one day. And anyway – it's all in here!" And she tapped her head to show Morva that everything she had found here was stored safely inside.

chapter Eight

"It's *Rani*!" shouted Kai, as she spotted her sister swimming towards their cave. "Rani – I've missed you so much!"

Their mother appeared, her long blonde hair swirling around her. "My darling!" she cried, rushing to greet her daughter.

"I'm so glad to be home, Mother!" Rani said, as they hugged.

Murdoch swam out of the cave with Pearl and shouted in delight as he saw his daughter again.

"You must come inside and tell us everything," Miriam said, taking her hand. "Where is Morva?"

"I've got so much to tell you," Rani gasped. "But first I want you to come with me. There's someone I'd like you to meet. You see . . . I found my brother. His name's Peri. I wanted to come and see you myself first, so I've left him with Octavius."

They all swam together to Octavius's cave.

"*Wow!*" exclaimed Kai, unable to believe her eyes. The royal carriage was parked outside and the dolphins were out of their harnesses, tucking into large helpings of Octavius's stew.

Inside the octopus's cave, they found Octavius telling Peri that he had guessed all along that Rani was a princess.

"A *princess?*" Kai said, gaping at her sister.

"It's a long story," Rani said, blushing.

"I think you'd better tell it to us right away," said Murdoch.

They all sat and listened as Rani and

Peri explained how they had been separated as babies long ago and that, while Rani was growing up in Tingle Reef, Peri had been brought up by their grandparents, the Mer-King and Queen.

"The Mer-King and Queen?" gasped Kai. "You mean . . . you mean, Rani really is a *princess*?"

Rani and Peri nodded.

Kai had non-stop questions for them after that – and so did everybody else. And they all wanted to see how the message-stone worked.

Rani let out a startled gasp as she opened the stone.

"What's wrong?" everyone asked.

"Nothing," Rani said, frowning. "It's just that *Morva* is inside." She looked at

Peri. "And s*he's* not family."

"I guess you must *think* of her like she is," her brother explained. "A message-stone can always pick up on these things!"

Rani thought about that for a moment. It was true that she had always *felt* very close to Morva. She started to smile as she looked into the stone again.

"Now I'll always be able to see her, even though she's not with me," Rani said happily.

"That's wonderful, darling!" her mother said, reaching out and stroking Rani's hair. "Now, children . . . I know this is all very exciting but it really is time for bed. You must be very tired – *especially* Rani and Peri!"

"Mother is a bit bossy, but you'll get used to her," Rani whispered to her brother.

"I think she's great!" Peri whispered back. "So is your father – *and* your sisters! You're so lucky to have *two* families!"

Rani just smiled. But she had a feeling that by the time Peri left Tingle Reef, *he* was going to have an extra family too.

Mermaid Magic

Gwyneth Rees

Rani came to Tingle Reef at the bottom of
the ocean when she was a baby mermaid –
she was found fast asleep in a seashell,
and nobody knows where she came from.

She's always been different with her bright red
hair and her amber eyes. But now strange things
keep happening to her – almost as if by magic!

Perhaps Rani's pet sea horse, Roscoe, and Octavius the
Octopus can help her find out what's going on . . .

Rani's Sea Spell

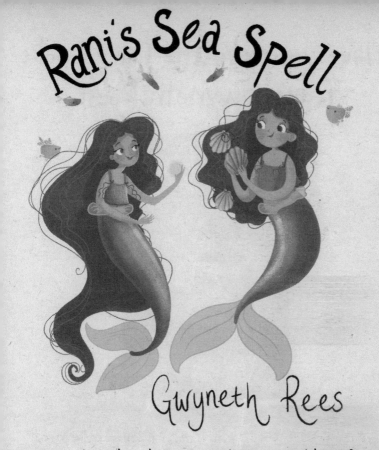

Gwyneth Rees

Rani's grandmother has invited Rani and her family to a party at her house in Deep Blue, a very long swim away from Rani's home in Tingle Reef.

When Grandmother gives Rani a beautiful amber necklace, she knows it must be special. She'll need to ask Morva the sea-witch about it when she gets home.

That's if she can make it past hungry sharks and grumpy whales! Perhaps it's time for a little magic . . .

Have you read the Fairy books from Gwyneth Rees?

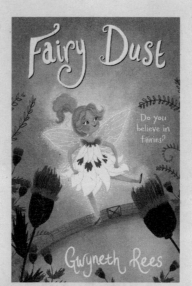

For older readers